I0691717

James Pillsbury Lane

Hampton Lane family memorial

A re-print of the address at the funeral of Dea. Joshua Lane of Hampton

James Pillsbury Lane

Hampton Lane family memorial
A re-print of the address at the funeral of Dea. Joshua Lane of Hampton

ISBN/EAN: 9783337269227

Printed in Europe, USA, Canada, Australia, Japan

Cover: Foto ©Raphael Reischuk / pixelio.de

More available books at **www.hansebooks.com**

IN MEMORIAM

A RE-PRINT

OF THE

ADDRESS AT THE FUNERAL

OF

DEA. JOSHUA LANE OF HAMPTON, N. H.

(Who was killed by lightning June 14, 1766.)

BY HIS SON,

DEA. JEREMIAH LANE of Hampton Falls.

WITH

SKETCHES OF HIS ANCESTRY AND FAMILIES

TO THE FOURTH GENERATION FROM

WILLIAM LANE OF BOSTON, MASS., 1651.

BY REV. JAS. P. LANE.

Printed by
LANE BROTHERS, NORTON, MASS.
1885.

At a meeting of the descendants of Dea. Joshua Lane, in the Town Hall at Hampton. N. H., August 18, 1885, plans were inaugurated to secure by subscription funds for the erection of a granite monument to mark the earliest known graves of ancestry in the ancient burial ground of Hampton. In carrying out those plans provision was made to re-print the funeral address entitled "A Tear of Lamentation," with sketches of ancestry and families to the fourth generation from William Lane of Boston. Mass., 1651. and to present a copy to every contributor of one dollar or more to the monument fund.

Committee to receive contributions and to erect the monument are

REV. J. W. LANE. No. Hadley. Mass.. *Chairman.*

J. G. LANE. Esq.. Manchester. *Secretary.*

G. W. LANE. Esq., Hampton. *Treasurer.*

MISS AUGUSTA ROBINSON. Exeter.

LEVI LANE. Esq.. Hampton Falls.

A

MEMORIAL,

AND TEAR OF

Lamentation,

WITH THE

IMPROVEMENT

Of the Death of Pious Friends,

Hampton Falls, July 17, 1766.

PORTSMOUTH, in *New Hampshire*;
Printed by D. & R. FOWLE, 1766.

PREFACE.

The following are some things which were suggesting to my mind, after the very heavy and melancholy tidings of the death of so dear a Friend: and being desirous, if possible, to do something in honour to so faithful, and good friend: that his remarkable example might not be forgotten, and buried with him; but that his memory might be preserved, and blessed.—I thought with myself, in the morning before his funeral. (not having had opportunity before) that I would then take my pen. and spend the former part of that day. in writing somewhat relative thereto: which after I had done. so far as time would allow; was somewhat thoughtful of offering it to my brethren. and sisters. at the funeral, if a convenient opportunity should present: but considering my inferior station in the brotherhood; concluded to defer it. but communicating it in part to my younger brother: was afterwards requested by my elder brother, to read the same; by which I was then embolden'd thereto.

But humbly do I offer it to you. my brethren and sisters; sensible of my own inferiority: and desiring that I may not be thought hereby. to pretend to any superiority among you. And I do hereby express. my grateful acknowledgements. of your kind acceptance of this my offering. and of your thus complying with the proposal.—And should this come under the inspection of others: and even of the learned. or whoever, of superior age. station or capacity: they are welcome to peruse it: but as it is not to be expected. neither do I pretend. to that correctness of speech. or composition, which might be expected from one of a liberal education: there is therefore desired, all that christian charity. and favourable allowance, that may appear needful.—I am sensible

that this, or a piece of this kind. might have been much better composed. by some worthy hand ; and perhaps even by the same unworthy. had there been time therefor, and a more deliberate contemplation thereon ; but this is what was then suggested to my mind ; altho' it is true as much more might have been added with equal propriety : but it is not for me to multiply words ; I am fearful lest I have exceeded herein already.

I have thought proper to style it a Tear of Lamentation, because composed with eyes full of tears, and a heart full of grief, by a very unworthy instrument,

Jeremiah Lane.

Hear ye Children the Instruction of a Father. *Prov*. 4. 1.

I go the way of all the Earth. be strong therefore and shew thy self a Man. 1*st. Kings* 2. 2.

And by it he being Dead, yet speaketh. *Heb*. 11. 4.

The Memory of the Just shall be Blessed. *Prov*. 10. 7.

The Glory of Children are their Fathers. *Prov*. 17. 6.

Sorrowing most of all for the Words which he spake, that they should see his Face no more. *Acts* 20. 38.

Then said Jesus, Go and do thou likewise. *Luke* 10. 37.

Hear O my son and Receive my sayings. *Prov*. 4. 10.

Give unto all their due, honour to whom honour is due. *Rom*. 13. 7.

Honour thy father and mother. *Matt*. 15. 4.

A

T E A R OF

Lamentation,

On the Death of Deacon *Joshua Lane*, of Hampton, who suddenly departed this life *June* 14, 1766; being struck Dead with the Lightning in the Entry of his House about Six o'clock in the Afternoon; Aged 70 Years.

In which is set forth something of his Character and Piety.

Being in a Brief Address, upon the very melancholly Occasion, to the mourning and justly lamenting Children at his Funeral *June* 16.

By One of the grieved Number.

In a Tear of LAMENTATION, with some Cordials of Consolation and Brief use of Application.

Printed for, and at the request of the Mourners.

A

TEAR of LAMENTATION, &c,

Beloved Brethren and Sisters,

ARE not each of us equally concern'd and even
in gratitude obliged to call upon ourselves and one
another, to unite in recollecting and setting forth in
our own and in our childrens view the *Character*,
and remarkable *Piety* of our honored dear FATHER,
who has been our crown, our glory. But now, is
this our crown taken from our head and this our
glory is departed from us.

It hath pleased God to make him an uncommon rich
Blessing unto us, and that to a good old age : But
now has call'd him home ; whereby we are unhappily
deprived of his agreeable company, and society ; of
his wholesome counsels and instructions which were
continually dropping from his graceful lips ; and of
his fervent prayers and supplications, and even
wrestlings with God at the throne of grace for us,
which we were always reaping the benefit of, which
we are to look upon as no small loss ; but that
as our defence is weakned upon this account, we
are to look upon ourselves, as doubly obliged to a
close application of ourselves to the throne of grace.
And now as we must see his pleasing face, his chearing

countenance. no more, nor hear his pleasant voice : let us in gratitude to this our pious and venerable deceased Friend ; in honour to God whose grace he was so eminently possess'd of and in honour to him who by the grace of God, was possess'd of so rich treasure, (altho' in an earthen vessel) let us even record his memory in our houses, that we and our children, and their children may see in after years, that we are the posterity of a pious ancestor ; thereby to enhance our obligation to piety, and that altho' he be dead he may be yet speaking.

We have abundant reason to have our breasts fill'd with affection towards this our beloved, departed Friend. whose breast was always big with affection towards us, his children, and posterity ; the evidences and expressions whereof, were continually flowing forth ; how tenderly have we been always imbrac'd as in his arms, with what love and delight was he always ready to hover us, as under his wing. How faithfully, and that to an uncommon degree, has he discharged his duty towards us, in giving us a religious and good education, (a bright talent for us to improve upon,) not only in his instructions. which were very extensive and frequent. and that upon all the fundamentals, and articles of christianity ; & upon all occurrences and occasions whatever ; but also in his exemplary walk and conduct. in exhibiting in his own life and example, (with the greatest care.) those things which he was instructing and exhorting ; how were religious expressions and heavenly conversation, interwoven with all his secular affairs, and worldly pursuits : and how careful always in his reserves, if it be God's will, by the leave of providence, if we

live and have our health. if nothing prevent. &c. always submitting his concerns to the will of God. and his wise disposals. No occurrence of divine providence pass'd unnoticed by him; always regarding the works of the Lord. and the operations of his holy hand. How evidently did there a spirit of piety, and of the fear of God, reign in his breast: what a fervent zeal did he ever maintain for the glory of God. How highly was the word of God priz'd by him, and how constant and universal was his daily attendance upon it: and how attentive was his ear always to the calls of God, in his word and providences. What a veneration did he continually maintain for the worship of God. both public and private: and how fervent in his prayers to God for grace, and for the interest of religion; to promote which seem'd to be his business while he was in the world. What a superiour high value did he always set upon Christ. who was indeed precious unto him, whose excellency he had discovered, and unto whom no doubt he was wedded; and by faith united: whose cause and interest was always near and dear to him. How close and humble was his constant walk with God. continually lamenting his imperfections. his defilement. and pollution by sin: the burden of which he always seem'd to be labouring under, and striving to have it subdued within him: and how precious were the promises of the gospel unto him; out of these breasts of consolation. did he seem by faith. to be continually drawing nourishment to his wearied soul. And altho' sin remained in him, yet thro' the grace of God. it was not suffered to reign. What

great use did he always make of Christ at the throne
of grace ; and superiour his expressions of his es-
teem of him : as well as at other times, occasionally :
on whom he depended, to carry on and to compleat his
salvation work : and how solicitous, always that he
might be found in him ; both living and dying,
which seemed to be his grand pursuit.   How dili-
gent and attentive, was he always found, in the constant use of the appointed means of grace : and
how earnest at the throne of grace. for the influences
of the holy spirit to accompany them : and did he
not cherish, the kind influences, of that heavenly
guest.   How conspicuous were the graces of the
holy spirit in exercise within him.   What faith,
how strong and unshaken in his belief of the gospel.
and things of a future state ; and how solicitous
always, that this grace might be continually in exercise, and increased, and strengthned within him :
what humility, what fervant zeal, what piety towards
God, did he maintain ; what charity toward his
fellow creatures : how constant in visiting those in
distress, and administring comfort and consolation
to them by his pious councils and exhortations :
and sympathizing with those under affliction, and
bereavement : and incessent in his prayers to God
for them : and taking notice of the necessities of
the poor, and lending a relieving hand.   How just
and conscientious, in his dealings and commerce ;
and how fearful of over reaching.   What temper-
ance, what meekness, what gravity, sobriety, and
heavenly mindedness, did he ever maintain ; what
care and circumspection in his walk, what watch-
fulness, what self denial and what a courteous be-

haviour, and amiable respectfulness did he shew toward all.

And now to return to our selves; with what delight, could we go and visit our dear Father; and how gladly were we entertained by him ; and when did we go away from him, without some useful instruction from his pious lips, which were continually forming that way: and how chearing were his fatherly visits to us, who were scattered. and settled from him ; and what could we not impart to so kind a friend ; who was always delighted in our happiness. and prosperity ; and who of us, but can witness for him, that he was constantly exhorting us, to receive all our mercies, as coming from God. and be sure to be concern'd to give him the glory, and the praise of all : And if at any time we were in affliction. how were his tender bowels yearning over us, and how certain always, of our Father's kind visits, and prayers. But now he has forsaken us, and very great indeed is the loss which we have sustain'd : But we mourn. not as those without hope ; let us not murmur or complain ; he is but gone to receive his reward, and no doubt a happy one : for saith Christ to his deciples and followers ; I go to prepare a place for you, and if I go and prepare a place for you, I will come again and receive you unto myself, that where I am, ye may be also, John 14. 2. And why should we desire to detain him any longer. It hath pleased God to make him a rich blessing unto us, it is he alone that has given him that grace which he has been possess'd of, and to him alone be the glory and the praise ; he has been pleased to continue him a long. as well as make him a rich blessing ; has he not

served God and his generation, according to the will of God; has he not improved his talents well: has he not accomplished his day, even three score years and ten. Has he not well accomplish'd his work: and has he not come to his grave, as a shock of corn in its season. (yea in its proper season) fully ripe; why then should we desire, that seeing the will of God is otherwise, why should we desire, that he should have to labour under the infirmities, and grievances of old age, and to grapple with its temptations. And as he has been set solitary of late, by the removal, and departure, of our honour'd dear mother; who has been his companion and mate, through the wilderness of this World, which they have passed together: in which it hath pleased God to smile upon them, and to bless them together; and altho' their beginning was small, yet thro' the smiles of Heaven, their latter end hath greatly increased; and great has been their happiness, and prosperity together. But as the happy pair have been broken, and parted, it could not be expected even upon this account, that he should enjoy that comfort, and satisfaction in his lonely state, as formerly; altho' as much as could be expected from a kind daughter, whom we have reason to respect, for her kindness and dutiful behaviour towards him. And as there has been of late (as it were) a cloud hanging over this church, the prosperity of which was always near his heart: and the present melancholy situation of which, has caus'd him much grief, and by reason of the difficulties, and temptations arising from hence, might he not be ready to say, my joy herein is much abated, altho' very de-

sirous of Zion's prosperity. So that had he lived
to spend his old age. until nature was worn out.
might it not be justly expected, that the shades of
evening were now drawing on; and that on many
accounts. might it not be said by him, my joy is departed: so that may not even these considerations.
serve in some measure, to abate and moderate our
grief.

And as to the manner. and outward circumstances
of his death, we have nothing to say (as many are
the ways in which the children of men are in-
discriminately call'd out of the world.) but that it
was the divine will and appointment: the arrow was
directed. and it hath fulfill'd the divine pleasure:
and if he was happily prepared, (as we have no
reason to doubt but he was) for he has been making
it his business to be continually ready for death. by
living as one whose time was always ready: and
especially if we consider with what reverance. awe.
and respect. he ever treated such seasons of thunder.
and lightning; as God's voice in the heavens: at
which times it was his practice to retire with his
family, from secular affairs and employments, and
to attend upon God's call herein: And here may we
not discover the kindness of God to him. (that seeing this was the way in which he was to be call'd out
of the world.) in thus giving him warning before-
hand, in causing his house over him to be rent and
shattered by the same voice of his terror.‡ might not
God have gracious designs herein. that he might
ever after. (in such seasons especially) be in a more
actual readiness; as it was always his earnest

‡ 26 *years ago.*

desire, and prayer, that he might be in an actual readiness for death, whenever, or however it might come,
suddenly or not: and were not the impressions of
God's former call, and visitation of this kind, now
fresh upon his grateful mind, as he was just making
mention of the same; and no doubt his heart was .
engaged in praising God, and contemplating his
wonderous works, while he was commemorating his
dealings towards him : Hence may we not infer that
God was dealing kindly, and graciously with him :
and may not we justly imagine from the long ex-
perience we have had of our Father's heavenly conduct, and reverend treatment of all God's calls and
dispensations ; may we not justly suppose that at
this present season, his soul was upon the wing, in
devout reflection and ejaculactions, while in a
moment, it was as a bird let out of its cage.   And
could we see through the whole scene of Providence,
no doubt we should see, that all things are ordered
for the best ; as they always are to them that love
and fear God, and walk in his ways.   And we know
that all things shall work together for good, to them
that love God, &c. Rom. 8. Forasmuch as ye know,
that your labour shall not be in vain in the Lord,
first Cor. 15. 58. O how great is thy goodness,
which thou hast laid up for them that fear thee,
which thou hast wrought for them that trust in thee,
before the sons of men, Psal. 31. 19. And nothing
shall be able to seperate them, from the love of God,
which is in Christ Jesus our Lord, Rom. 8. 39.
May we not depend upon it, that all things are ordered in infinite wisdom and in infinite goodness, and
that for the best in the whole, to bring about God's

infinitely wise designs, and purposes. And that when the scene is opened, we shall be abundantly satisfied : What I do. thou knowest not now, but thou shalt know hereafter, John 13. 7. So that have we not reason to acquiesce, in all God's dealings, and dispensations, towards his children. as being for the best. And if this our beloved friend, was thus prepared, and thus ready for death, what a quick and (may we not suppose) easy passage was he favour'd with ; so that he had not the agonies of a death bed, to labour under : if ye loved me ye would rejoice, because I go to the Father. John 14. 28. And altho' he go to Heaven in a fiery chariot. yet no doubt safe the conveyance, and perhaps the more so, by the quickness of the passage : altho' we, with Elisha have reason to cry, my Father. my Father, the chariot of Israel, and the horsemen thereof. 2d Kings 2. 12 So that considering all things, as to outward circumstances, have we not reason to say. that God hath dealt graciously, and mercifully with him.

And now, may it please God, to let the spirit of his dear, deceased servant. rest upon us his children, and posterity : that spirit of piety, of the fear of God, that spirit of faith, and zeal of humility, meekness and heavenly mindedness, and shall we not be solicitously seeking after these ornaments : and carefully cherish all the motions and designs arising within us, (from a grateful remembrance of this our deceased friend) to follow, and imitate him, wherein he imitated Christ, that perfect pattern, and great exemplar, whom he took for his pattern, for his guide, his saviour, and his all. And of whom

might it not be said, that he followed the Lamb, whithersoever he goeth, as, Rev. 14. 4. And may we not, (thro' grace) confidently hope, that he is now with the Lamb; For he that overcometh. the same shall be clothed in white raiment, and I will not blot out his name out of the book of life, but I will confess his name before my Father and before his angels. And to him will I grant. to sit with me in my throne, even as I also overcame and am set down with my Father in his throne, Rev. 3. 5. 21. Let us honour God, and his grace. and honour this our dear, deceased friend; by exhibiting in our lives. whatever was amiable. and virtuous in his life. Have we not had a careful Guide, to shew us our way and set us out therein; and that has carefully gone before us in it: and herein are not our obligations to piety, very great: for unto whom much is given, of them much will be required. And now has not our father left us, in a day of great degeneracy, and corruption; is not our way hedged up with enemies, with snares, with temptations, with errors and delusions. Let us then strive to stem the current of vice. and be seeking after heavenly wisdom, and prudence in our way; taking the word of God for our rule, Christ for our pattern: and let us stand steadfast in the faith, of the gospel; seeking diligently, to be well established, and built up in Christ. Are not the walls of Jerusalem now greatly weaken'd, is there not a sore breach made therein, and is it not besieged with enemies: let us then take our father's place. even upon Jerusalem's walls, and stand in the gap in Jerusalem's cause, for her desolation is threatened.

We know not what calamities our pious friends even our own parents may be taken from. Our father, and our mother, have now in a short time forsaken us: shall not we their children, and posterity, arise up and call them blessed: and carefully follow their good examples, and recollect, and hearken to, their wholesome councils and instructions: That now their bed together is in the dust. may we be concern'd to make good our leaders ground; to improve our talents, and not keep them hid: let us be followers of those, who thro' faith and patience. are gone to inherit the promises. Let us act the part while we are upon the stage, for the time is short, and it is at hand, that he that is unjust. shall be unjust still. and he that is righteous. shall be righteous still. &c. Rev. 22. 11. One generation passeth away, (and it is quickly brought about) and another generation followeth after; shall we not then, be laying up in store. a good foundation against the time to come; shall it not be our business, to lay up treasure in Heaven, that when we also must leave the world, we may have occasion to rejoice, that we are going to possess our treasure. having it laid up in Heaven. in Christ's treasure-house, and not to mourn. that we are going to leave our treasure behind. having it laid up in this world, which is not our home, but only our stage, to act our part upon. Let us then use the world, according to the relation it stands in unto us; which is only to serve our passage thro' it: and solicitously be seeking after the qualifications of true citizens of Zion; that at length we may (thro' grace) join the happy society, which surround the throne of God. celebrating the praise of God, and the Lamb forever and ever.   J. L.

Happy the company that's gone,
From cross to crown from thrall to throne,
How loud they sing upon the shore,
To which they sail'd in heart before.

Death is to them a sweet repose,
The bud was op' to shew the rose,
The cage was broke to let them fly,
And build their happy nest on high,

DEACON JOSHUA LANE, was born O. S. June 6, 1696, and died June 14, N. S. 1766. Aged 3 days short of 70 years. —— BATHSHEBA, his wife, who was formerly BATHSHEBA ROBIE, was born O. S. Aug. 2. 1696. Died N. S. April 13, 1765, aged 68 years & 8 months.——They were married Dec. 24, 1717, in the 22d year of their age. —Their abode together in the married state was 47 years, 3 months and 8 days.—Their departure was within 14 months and 1 day of each other.—The number of their children was 16, 13 of which survived, and followed them to their graves.—The number of their grandchildren, at the grandfather's decease 60, 52 of which were then living, and 3 of which were born after the grandmother's decease. —The number of children in law, or by marriage 13, 12 of which survive.—The number of the great grandchildren 4, 3 of which are living, and one of which was born after the great grand mother's decease—The number of grand children by marriage 2.

The number of the whole Family of children, grand children, children and grand children by marriage, and great grand children 95. 82 of which survive.

F I N I S.

NOTE.

The following corrections are made in writing on a copy which has come down from Jeremiah Lane, the author, and were doubtless made by him after it was printed.

"Some small correction and addition, the copy not being thoroughly examined and finished as it ought to have been—its coming to the Press unexpectedly—which addition is here discoverable being made with the pen.

The addition is on Page 3rd at the bottom.

Give unto all their due. honour to whom honour is due. Rom. 13. 7.

Honour thy Father and Mother. Matt. 15. 4. and in page 6 *all.* (This is inserted between 'upon' and 'occurrences' "upon *all* occurrences")

And in page 10 the second line from the bottom. the word printed we is altered as it was intended to *he.* ("Might *he* not be ready to say, etc.")

These corrections have been made in this Reprint.

THE ANCESTRY

OF

Dea. Joshua Lane of Hampton, N.

(Who was killed by lightning June 14, 1766.)

AND FAMILIES

TO THE

FOURTH GENERATION

FROM

WILLIAM LANE OF BOSTON, MASS., 1651.

Among early settlers in New England in the 17th century were a dozen or more of the name **Lane**. Attempts to trace pedigree to a common ancestor have been but partially successful. Kinship between several of them has been discovered, and much valuable information respecting nearly all of them and their descendants for several generations has been collected. We shall be glad to receive any information that may aid in completing the record. The name was quite common in England. Scotland. and Wales at the time of the first immigrations to America. Tradition says that it originated among the Huguenots of France in the 16th century and designated a clan of wool-growers, called "the Lanes" from *Lana*, the Latin for wool.

J. P. L.

Norton, Mass., Sept. 8, 1885.

We have given dates as originally written. i. e. in Old Style before 1752, excepting that dates between Jan. 1 and March 25 are given with the single instead of the double year.   To change Old Style to New Style ten days should be added to all dates before 1699, and eleven days should be added to all dates between 1699 and 1752.

WILLIAM LANE OF BOSTON, MASS., 1651.

William Lane was a resident of Boston, Mass., in 1651. It is not known when he came. Tradition says he came from Scotland. It is also said he was a kinsman of **William Lane** of Dorchester, Mass., who came in 1635 from Norfolk Co., England with his adult family, **Andrew** and **George** and four daughters, who were among the original settlers in Hingham, Mass. Also that he was a kinsman of **Job, James** and **Edward Lane**, three brothers from Yorkshire, England, who settled in Billerica (now Bedford), and Malden, Mass., Gloucester, Mass., and Falmouth (now Portland), Me.

His wife was **Mary** ———.

Their children were

   i. **Samuel**, b. 23 Jan. 1651.

   ii. **John**, b. 5 Feb. 1653.

   iii. **Mary**, b. 15 May 1656.

The mother died, according to the Boston records, 2 May 1656. Evidently an error. The correct date was probably 22 May 1656.

The father married 21 Aug. 1656, **Mary Brewer**, daughter of Thomas Brewer of Roxbury, Mass.

Their children were

    iv. **Sarah**, b. 15 June 1657.

    v. **William**, b. 1 Oct. 1659.

    vi. **Elizabeth**, b. 3 Feb. 1661.

    vii. **Ebenezer**, b. 21 March 1666.

NOTES.

But little is known of William Lane. He was a cordwainer or shoemaker by trade, and tradition says was an industrious and worthy citizen. He was admitted freeman 6 May 1657.

Thomas Brewer was of English origin and among the early inhabitants of Ipswich. Mass., afterwards removing to Roxbury. He died in Hampton. N.H., at the residence of his son-in-law, Thomas Webster, called "goodman Brewer."

II.

WILLIAM LANE OF HAMPTON. N. H.

William Lane, son of William and Mary (Brewer) Lane, born in Boston, 1 Oct. 1659, married. 21 June 1680, **Sarah Webster**, daughter of Thomas and Sarah (Brewer) Webster, born in Hampton, 22 Jan. 1660. They lived in Boston until after the birth of their first child, when they removed to Hampton where he died, 14 Feb. 1749. She died in Hampton, 6 Jan. 1745.

Their children were

    i. **John**, b. 17 Feb. 1685.

    ii. **Sarah**, b. 6 Nov. 1688.

    iii. **Elizabeth**, b. 12 July 1691.

iv. **Abigail**, b. 9 Dec. 1693.

v. **Joshua**, b. 6 June 1696.

vi. **Samuel**, b. 4 June 1698.

vii. **Thomas**, b. 8 June 1701.

NOTES.

William Lane was a tailor by trade. He had a grant of ten acres from the town of Hampton, on which he built his house. near the spot where the Hampton Academy has stood for many years. Here he lived and reared his family. carrying on his trade successfully. Though not wealthy, he was in comfortable circumstances and a worthy citizen. His name appears on the list of members of the Second church in Boston, 1 March 1681, and that of his wife, 29 May following.

Thomas Webster was a son of Thomas and Margery Webster, born in Ormsby, Norfolk Co., England, where he was baptized 20 Nov. 1631. His father died in April 1634. His mother married William Godfrey. In 1638 he came with his mother and step-father to Watertown, Mass. They removed to Hampton, N. H. Here Mr. Godfrey was chosen Deacon and held the office till his death, 25 March 1671. The son married 29 May 1657 Sarah Brewer, daughter of Thomas Brewer and sister of Mary Brewer, wife of William Lane of Boston. They lived in Hampton on the "Drake road," near "Webster's brook," and he owned a part of "the small gains." He was the ancestor of the distinguished statesman of Marshfield, Mass., Hon. Daniel Webster. See N. E. Gen. Reg., Vol. IX, p. 159.

III.

DEA. JOSHUA LANE, OF HAMPTON, N. H.

Joshua Lane, son of William and Sarah (Webster) Lane, born in Hampton 6 June 1696 married 24 Dec. 1717, **Bathsheba Robie**, daughter of Samuel and Mary Robie, born in Hampton, 2 Aug. 1696. They lived in Hampton, on a farm on the road to North Hampton, about half a mile from the R. R. Depot. In addition to the care of his farm he carried on his trade of tanner and shoemaker.

Their children were

    i. **Samuel**, b. 6 Oct. 1718.

    ii. **Mary**, b. 7 Feb. 1720.

    iii. **Joshua**, b. 16 May 1721, d. 30 May 1723.

    iv. **William**, b. 11 June 1723.

    v. **Joshua**, b. 8 July 1724.

    vi. **Josiah**, b. 8 July 1724. d. 22 July 1729.

    vii. **John**, b. 14 Feb. 1726.

    viii. **Sarah**, b. 3 Dec. 1727.

    ix. **Bathsheba**, b. 6 June 1729, d. 5 Sept. 1757.

    x. **Isaiah**, b. 21 Dec. 1730.

    xi. **Jeremiah**, b. 10 March 1732.

    xii. **Ebenezer**, b. 26 Sept. 1733.

    xiii. **Abigail**, b. 13 Nov. 1734.

    xiv. **Elizabeth**, b. 25 May 1736.

    xv. **Josiah**, b. 19 May 1738.

    xvi. **Anne**, b. 24 March 1741.

NOTES.

Joshua Lane united with the church in Hampton with his wife 10 March 1718. At this time he signed an "Act of Consecration," which is still preserved in his handwriting, which breathed the spirit of that earnest piety which was characteristic of him in all his subsequent life. Not long after uniting with the church he was chosen Deacon and held the office till death. In every relation of life his character was eminent for christian virtue. He was highly esteemed in the community and exerted a wide and salutary influence. He was specially happy in his family. His wife was a fit companion and help-meet, heartily and wisely aiding him in the training of their children to habits of industry and piety. His death was a sudden and unexpected event. A heavy thunderstorm had nearly passed over, when, on stepping to the front door of the house, he was instantly killed by lightning. This was about six o'clock in the afternoon 14 June 1766. His wife had died 13 April 1765.

Samuel Robie was a son of Samuel Robie, who came from Yorkshire, England as early as 1639, where he was born 12 Feb. 1619 in "Castle Dunnington," the family seat.

Bathsheba Lane, the daughter who died 15 Sept. 1757 unmarried, united with the church at 15 years of age, 15 July 1744, and was a worthy and useful member.

Excepting this daughter and the two who died in infancy, the children all lived to adult age and had families.

The late Ebenezer Lane, Esq., of Pittsfield, N.H. left in writing a record of his personal recollections of the family fifty years before, as follows: —

"They were all persons of highly respectable character. Eight sons lived to a good old age. They were all mechanics and farmers. Six of them were tanners and shoemakers, one a tailor, and one a carpenter and cabinet maker. Their shops adjoined their houses so that they could enter them without going into the open air. They all had farms which they cultivated in connection with their trades. Their work was of the best quality and commanded the highest prices in the market. None of them were poor, nor were any of them rich, realizing the condition of Agur's prayer. All were men of steady habits, regular and prudent in their intercourse with the world, strictly honest in their dealings, careful in making promises and faithful in keeping them. I once saw five of them together at my father's house in Stratham. They were truly a patriarchal looking band, neatly clad in the costumes of those times. They were easy in their manners and moderately sociable, not inclined to loquacity, but talking enough to make conversation agreeable, entertaining and instructive."

I. **Samuel Lane** m. 24 Dec. 1741 Mary James. Lived in Stratham. Was selectman and town-clerk for many years. Was a member of the Provincial Assembly which met in Exeter, 1776. Was deacon and elder in the church. Had eight children. The mother died 30 July 1769. He m. 22 June 1774, Rachel Colcord widow of Gideon Colcord of Newmarket. He died 29 Dec. 1806. She died 18 Jan. 1813. The children all lived to adult age and had families in Stratham, Newmarket, Northwood, Sanbornton and vicinity. Dea. E. J. Lane of Dover and Rev. J. W. Lane of North Hadley. Mass. descended from Samuel Lane.

II. **Mary Lane** m. 7 Feb. 1740 Jabez James. Lived in Hampton. Had three children. He died

18 June 1752.   She m. 20 May 1755 Jonathan Shaw. Had four children.   He died 30 May 1780. Hon. Tristram Shaw of Exeter, M. C. from New Hampshire, was a grandson.

iv. William Lane m. 13 Feb. 1746 Rachel Ward. Lived in Hampton. Was deacon in the church. Had eight children, five of whom lived to adult age : four had families in Hampton and Deerfield ; one died unmarried. He died 20 Dec. 1802.   She died 10 Dec. 1805.

v. Joshua Lane m. 16 Dec. 1747 Ruth Batchelder. Lived in Hampton till 1762 and removed to Poplin (now Fremont) where he had a farm next that of Joseph Godfrey near Epping, said to have been the best in town, and also carried on trade of carpenter and cabinet-maker. He was a man of the strictest integrity and christian virtue and eminent as a citizen. Had ten children, seven of whom lived to adult age and had families in Candia, Deerfield, Raymond, Epping, and Poplin. They were all persons of excellent character and influence. He died 13 Jan. 1794. She survived her husband many years and passed the evening of her life in a serene and happy old age among her children. She died 14 June 1812.

One of the sons of Joshua Lane was John Lane, who m. Hannah Godfrey, daughter of Joseph Godfrey, and lived in Candia. He held a prominent position in town affairs and was eminent for his salutary influence in all relations. He had eleven children, several of whom were equally prominent in character and influence. Mrs. Emily, wife of Ex-Gov. Frederic Smythe, of Manchester, Mrs. Harriet N. (Lane) Eaton, of Merrimac, Rev. Jas. H. Fitts, of So. Newmarket, John G. Lane, Esq., of Manchester, the writer of these sketches, and his

sons, the printers, of Norton, Mass. are descendants of John Lane of Candia. Miss Augusta Robinson. of Exeter, is descendant from another son of Joshua. Isaiah Lane of Fremont.

VII. John Lane m. Hannah Dow. Lived in Kensington. Had eight children, six of whom lived to adult age and had families in Kensington, Deerfield. and Sanbornton. He was a member of the church in Hampton. He died in Kensington, 21 March 1811. She died there, 10 Sept. 1775.

VIII. Sarah Lane m. 1 Jan. 1747 Dea. Jonathan Weare of Seabrook. Had five children, all of whom lived to adult age and had families. She died 8 June 1784.

X. Isaiah Lane m. 24 July 1755 Sarah Perkins. We do not know that he had children. He died 23 Oct. 1815. She died 16 March 1823.

XI. Jeremiah Lane m. 18 Jan. 1759 Mary Sanborn. Lived in Hampton Falls. where he was Deacon. He was a man of cultivated taste. eminent as a penman and artist, the writer of the "Tear of Lamentation." Had seven children, five of whom lived to adult age and had families in Pittsfield, Chichester and Hampton Falls. Levi Lane Esq. of Hampton Falls is a descendant of Dea. Jeremiah Lane.

XII. Ebenezer Lane m. 16 Nov. 1757 Huldah Fogg. Lived in Hampton. Had seven children, five of whom lived to adult age and had families. He died 20 May 1796. She died 13 July 1814.

XIII. Abigail Lane m. 19 Dec. 1754 Thomas Berry. Had nine children, six of whom lived to adult age and had families. She died 9 Nov. 1826. He died 14 March 1799.

XIV. Elizabeth Lane m. 19 Nov. 1782 John Robie. We do not know that she had children. She died 1 Sept. 1806. He died 16 Nov. 1794.

xv. Josiah Lane m. 26 Nov. 1760 Betsey Perkins. Lived in Hampton on the homestead estate inherited from his father, he paying bequests to the other children. Had twelve children, eight of whom lived to adult age and had families. The family of Reuben L. Seavey, living on the homestead in Hampton, are descendants of Josiah Lane.

xvi. Anne Lane m. 28 Feb. 1760 Joseph Johnson. of Hampton, who removed to Readfield, Me. We do not know that she had children. She died 2 Feb. 1780. He died in Nov. 1794.

We have names and genealogical records of grandchildren and many of their descendants for several generations. We would be very glad to receive information from any source that may aid in completing the records. We will be very grateful for any corrections of errors that may have come into the accounts here given. We earnestly request all persons interested to forward to the writer any items, genealogical or biographical, that they may have, which may be of value in completing this family history.

www.ingramcontent.com/pod-product-compliance
Lightning Source LLC
Chambersburg PA
CBHW032140270626
47172CB00009B/644